The Grumpy, Grumpy Grandpa

By Lenore Marchese

I dedicate this book to my very dear husband, John, the wind beneath my wings, to Andrea and Marissa, our wonderful daughters, and to my beloved grandkids, Louie, Carlo, Sophia and Lily.

Once upon a time, there was a grandpa named John. He was a very nice man, but he was a grumpy, grumpy grandpa.

On Monday, he ate his favorite lunch, a hotdog. But John was still a grumpy, grumpy grandpa.

On Tuesday he went fishing with his friend Sam. He caught a flounder fish. But John was still a grumpy, grumpy grandpa,

On Wednesday, he went to his club where he saw his friends. But John was still a grumpy, grumpy grandpa.

On Thursday, he went to the beach he loved. It was a beautiful sunny day good for sunbathing which John loved to do.

But John was still a grumpy, grumpy grandpa.

On Friday, John listened to jokes on his computer.
But John was still a grumpy, grumpy grandpa.

On Saturday, he went out for his favorite breakfast of bacon and eggs. But John was still a grumpy, grumpy grandpa.

He even had his favorite sandwich of salami and cheese with mustard and mayo for lunch. But John was still a grumpy, grumpy grandpa.

Then on Sunday, things changed for John.

The doorbell rang and John was in for a very special treat.

First, his two little grandsons, Louie and Carlo,
came to visit John.

Then his two little granddaughters, Sophia and Lily came too.

Each of them gave John seven sweet kisses and
two big hugs.

Then they each gave him a beautiful big smile and
suddenly John's heart began to SMILE.

KABOOM!!!!!!!!!

All of a sudden, John was not a grumpy, grumpy grandpa anymore.

His big frown turned into a big smile.

Then John became a very happy, happy grandpa.

And he still is!!!

About the Author.......

Lenore Marchese is the wife of John for 47 years. They have two daughters, Andrea and Marissa, and four grandchildren, Louie, Carlo, Sophia and Lily. She is a retired elementary science teacher and she was an adjunct professor. She currently works with developmentally disabled adults teaching them to express themselves through poetry and writing. She and John feel privileged and blessed to care for their grandchildren and to spend as much time with them.

All the proceeds from the sale of this book will be donated to Operation Smile, a wonderful organization whose mission is to provide reconstructive surgery to children of third world countries who are disfigured from birth. Lenore believes every child deserves a chance to smile.